This book belongs to:

....

Note to parents and carers

Read it yourself is a series of classic, traditional tales, written in a simple way to give children a confident and successful start to reading.

Each book is carefully structured to include many high-frequency words that are vital for first reading. The sentences on each page are supported closely by pictures to help with reading, and to offer lively details to talk about.

The books are graded into four levels that progressively introduce wider vocabulary and longer stories as a reader's ability grows.

Ideas for use

- Ask how your child would like to approach reading at this stage. Would he prefer to hear you read the story first, or would he like to read the story to you and see how he gets on?

- Help him to sound out any words he does not know.

- Developing readers can be concentrating so hard on the words that they sometimes don't fully grasp the meaning of what they're reading. Answering the puzzle questions on pages 46 and 47 will help with understanding.

For more information and advice, visit www.ladybird.com/readityourself

Level 3 is ideal for children who are developing reading confidence and stamina, and who are eager to read longer stories with a wider vocabulary.

Special features:

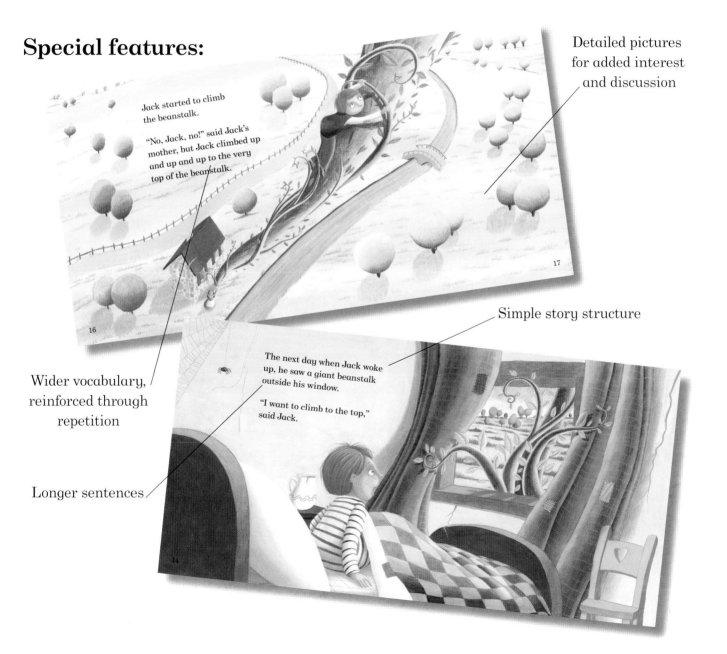

Detailed pictures for added interest and discussion

Jack started to climb the beanstalk.

"No, Jack, no!" said Jack's mother, but Jack climbed up and up and up to the very top of the beanstalk.

17

16

Simple story structure

The next day when Jack woke up, he saw a giant beanstalk outside his window.

"I want to climb to the top," said Jack.

Wider vocabulary, reinforced through repetition

Longer sentences

14

Educational Consultant: Geraldine Taylor

A catalogue record for this book is available from the British Library

Published by Ladybird Books Ltd
80 Strand, London, WC2R 0RL
A Penguin Company

2 4 6 8 10 9 7 5 3
© LADYBIRD BOOKS LTD MMX
Ladybird, Read It Yourself and the Ladybird Logo are registered or
unregistered trade marks of Ladybird Books Limited.

ISBN: 978-1-40930-353-4

Printed in China

Jack and the Beanstalk

Illustrated by Laura Barella

Jack and his mother were very poor. All they had was one cow.

One day, Jack's mother said, "Go and sell our cow and bring the money back to me."

Jack took the cow away to sell.
On the way he met a man who
wanted to buy the cow.

"I have no money," said the man. "But I will give you five magic beans for your cow."

"All right," said Jack, and he gave the man his cow.

11

Jack took the beans back to his mother. She was very angry.

"These beans are no good to us," she said. And she threw the beans out of the window.

The next day when Jack woke up, he saw a giant beanstalk outside his window.

"I want to climb to the top," said Jack.

Jack started to climb
the beanstalk.

"No, Jack, no!" said Jack's
mother, but Jack climbed up
and up and up to the very
top of the beanstalk.

Jack saw a giant castle
with a giant door. When
he opened the door he saw
a giant woman.

"Look out!" said the woman.
"My husband is coming.
He will eat you up!"

"Fee fi fo fum, watch out everyone, HERE I COME," roared the giant.

"You must hide," said the woman. And she hid Jack in a cupboard.

The giant came in and sat down at the table with some giant bags of money. He started to count his money. Jack watched him from inside the cupboard.

23

Soon, the giant fell asleep.
Jack came out of the cupboard
and took all the money.
Then he climbed down the
beanstalk, and gave the
money to his mother.

Not long after, Jack wanted
to climb the beanstalk again.

"No, Jack, no!" said his
mother. But Jack said,
"I must."

Jack saw the giant woman again.

"Look out!" she said. "My husband is angry because his money has been stolen."

"Fee fi fo fum, watch out everyone, HERE I COME!" roared the giant.

"You must hide in the cupboard," said the woman.

The giant came in and sat down at the table. He had with him a magic hen. The magic hen laid golden eggs.

Very soon, the giant fell asleep.
Jack came out of the cupboard
and took the hen. Then he
climbed down the beanstalk.

The next day, Jack climbed the beanstalk again. At the top of the beanstalk, Jack saw the giant woman.

"Look out!" said the woman. "My husband is angry because his hen and his money have been stolen."

"Fee fi fo fum, watch out everyone, HERE I COME!" roared the giant.

"You must hide in the cupboard again," said the woman.

The giant came in with a magic harp. He sat down at the table and the harp started to play.

Soon, the giant fell asleep. Jack came out of the cupboard and took the harp. Then he started to climb down the beanstalk.

"Run away!" said the woman. "The giant is behind you!"

Jack climbed down the beanstalk with the angry giant behind him. When Jack was at the bottom, his mother cut down the beanstalk.

CRASH! And that was the end of the giant.

Now Jack and his mother
were not poor, and they lived
happily ever after.

How much do you remember about the story of Jack and the Beanstalk? Answer these questions and find out!

- How many magic beans were there?

- What did Jack's mother do with the magic beans?

- What was at the top of the beanstalk?

- Where did Jack hide in the castle?

- Can you remember two of the things Jack took from the giant?

Look at the different story sentences and match them to the people who said them.

"Fee fi fo fum."

"Run away! The giant is behind you!"

"I will give you five magic beans for your cow."

"These beans are no good to us!"

"I want to climb to the top."

Read it yourself
with Ladybird

Collect all the titles in the series.